No MORE KISSING!

Emma Chichester Clark

for Rodney

This paperback edition first published in 2018 by Andersen Press Ltd.
First published in Great Britain in 2001 by Andersen Press Ltd.,
20 Vauxhall Bridge Road, London SW1V 2SA.
Text and Illustration copyright © Emma Chichester Clark, 2001.
The rights of Emma Chichester Clark to be identified as the author
and illustrator of this work have been asserted by her in accordance
with the Copyright, Designs and Patents Act, 1988.
All rights reserved.
Colour separated in Switzerland by Photolitho AG, Zürich.
Printed and bound in Malaysia.

10   9   8   7   6   5   4   3   2   1

British Library Cataloguing in Publication Data available.
ISBN 978 1 78344 585 1

It goes on
everywhere,

all over the place,
especially mummies kissing babies.

I wish no one had invented kissing.

And I wish no one
would kiss ME,

especially…

people
I don't KNOW!

My family do it too,
all the time.

They kiss Hello,
then they kiss Goodbye.

They kiss Good Morning.

they kiss Good Night.

When my cousin, Mimi, hurt her finger, everyone had to kiss it better. She loves kissing. She'll kiss anything…

... but not ME!
My mum is always telling us to kiss
and make up.

I've told all my
family — my mum,
my dad, my grandma,
all my cousins, my
uncle and my aunts...

But it makes

no difference

at all !

I'm glad I'm not
a baby any more.

They get more kisses than anyone.

It doesn't matter whose baby they are, or how much they squeak or squeal...

...or screech, everyone wants to kiss them. So I knew what was going to happen...

...when our new baby came.
He screamed his head off.

The more they Kissed him,
the more he screamed.
The more he screamed,
the more they Kissed him.

"STOP!" I shouted.

"Can't you see he
doesn't like it?"

"Perhaps you'd like to hold him?"
asked my grandma.

First, I showed him my aeroplane,
but he just cried.

Next, I made funny faces,
but he cried even more.
Then, I juggled some bananas.

He cried and cried and cried.
Now what shall I do? I wondered.
"What's the matter, little brother?"
His eyes popped open.
We looked at each other, eye to eye.

"Little brother," I said, and he smiled.
And then a weird thing happened,
by mistake I think. I kissed him.

It was lucky no one was looking.